JOURNEY TO STAR WARS: THE FORCE AWAKENS

# STAR WARS®
# SHIPS OF THE GALAXY

Written by Benjamin Harper

studio fun

A READER'S DIGEST COMPANY

White Plains, New York • Montréal, Québec • Bath, United Kingdom

# DROID CONTROL SHIP

Droid Control Ships were gigantic cargo haulers modified in secret to house giant droid armies. The Trade Federation's notorious craft were also modified for battle with approximately 42 deadly quad lasers. These ships carried 6,520 armored assault tanks (AATs), 550 multi-troop transports (MTTs), 50 landing ships, 1,500 droid starfighters, and a vast army of battle droids.

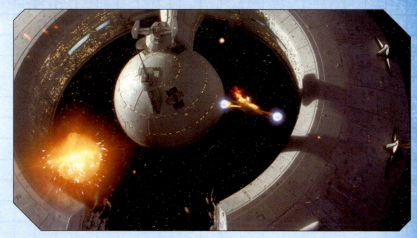

Giant circular hangars and sensor arrays encircled the command centerspheres. Central control computers designed to radio commands to the massive droid armies from remote locations kept Trade Federation officials in command of battles but far away from any danger.

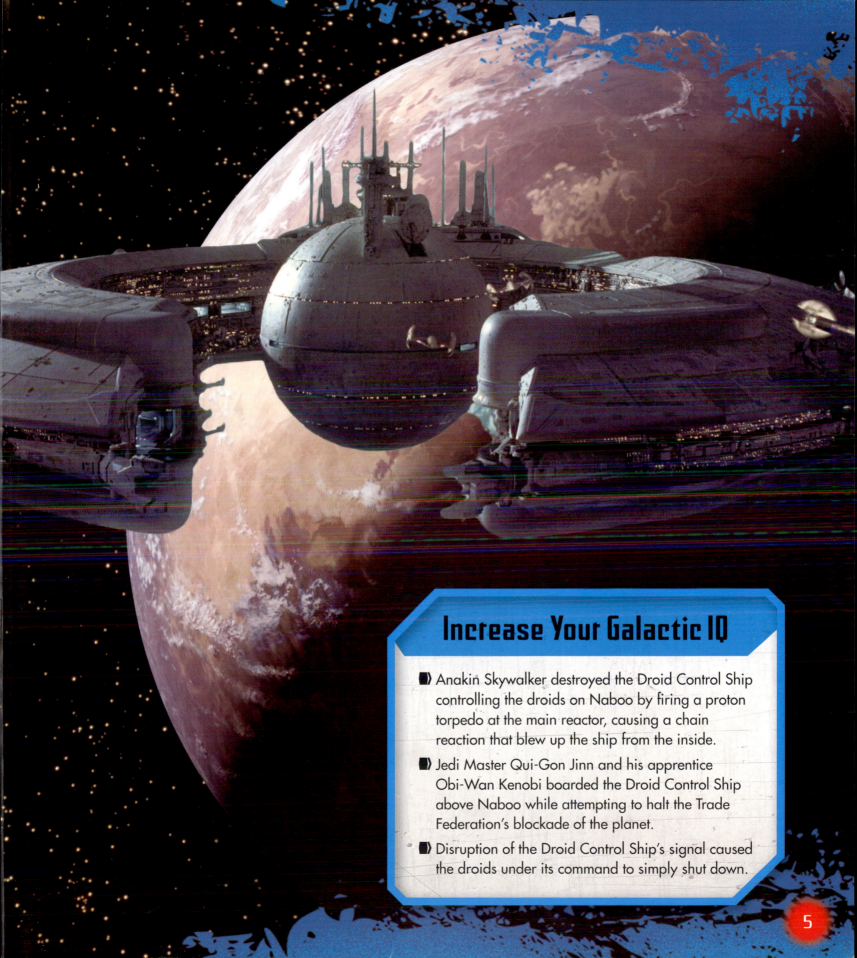

## Increase Your Galactic IQ

◗ Anakin Skywalker destroyed the Droid Control Ship controlling the droids on Naboo by firing a proton torpedo at the main reactor, causing a chain reaction that blew up the ship from the inside.

◗ Jedi Master Qui-Gon Jinn and his apprentice Obi-Wan Kenobi boarded the Droid Control Ship above Naboo while attempting to halt the Trade Federation's blockade of the planet.

◗ Disruption of the Droid Control Ship's signal caused the droids under its command to simply shut down.

# SITH INFILTRATOR

This devious looking vehicle was Darth Maul's personal starship, used to carry out dark missions for his Sith Master. The Sith Infiltrator was particularly dastardly because it included a cloaking device, allowing it to disappear from any tracking systems and slip by unnoticed.

The ship was secretly modified to enhance its abilities. It had six deadly laser cannons—four were included in its original design, and two were added at a later date. The Sith Infiltrator's experimental ion engines required radiator fins on the ship's wings to be open during flight to expel heat.

## Increase Your Galactic IQ

- Darth Maul used the Sith Infiltrator to track Queen Amidala to Tatooine. There he released sinister probe droids that scattered to various settlements to seek out the Queen.

- Darth Maul kept a speeder bike aboard the Sith Infiltrator for traveling short distances from the ship in a hurry.

- Maximum speed: 1,180 kilometers per hour (kph)

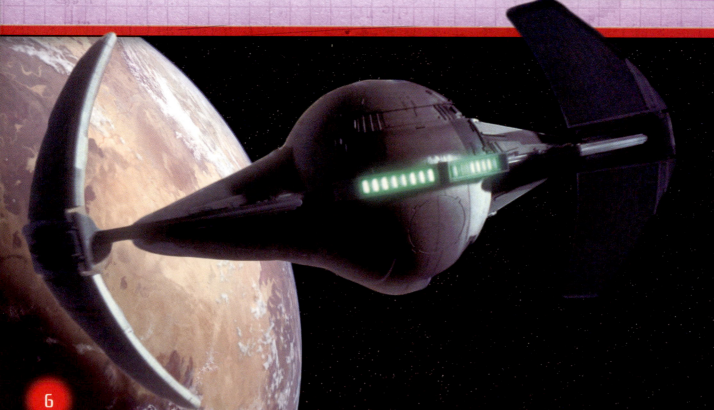

# QUEEN AMIDALA'S
# ROYAL STARSHIP

This unique craft was designed by the Theed Palace Space Vessel Engineering Corps, with a gleaming chromium surface to signify the presence of royalty. Engaged primarily to escort the Queen around Naboo, the glimmering starship also flew on official off-world business.

The frame was designed on Naboo but the sublight and hyperdrive engines were Nubian. The Naboo were a peaceful people, and the Royal Starship was constructed without any weapons. It was equipped, however, with deflector shields in case of attack.

## Increase Your Galactic IQ

- When the Trade Federation attacked the Queen's Royal Starship and damaged its deflector shields, R2-D2 repaired the shields and the ship slipped past the blockade.
- Jedi Master Qui-Gon Jinn found a replacement engine in Mos Espa on Tatooine when the hyperdrive was damaged—he won the engine from Watto in a bet on the Boonta Eve Podrace.
- The astromech droid bay housed eight droids ready for various tasks.
- Length: 76 meters

# NABOO N-1 STARFIGHTER

Theed Palace Space Vessel Engineering Corps created this sleek, shimmering fighter for the Royal Naboo Security Forces. The design complemented the elegant Royal Starship, complete with buffed chromium finishes on its forward surfaces.

Used as an escort for the ruling monarch of Naboo, this single-pilot craft had a central rat-tail that acted as a power charger, receiving energy from generators when not in use. The ship possessed two laser cannons and proton torpedoes, and two outer finials that served as heat sinks for the engines.

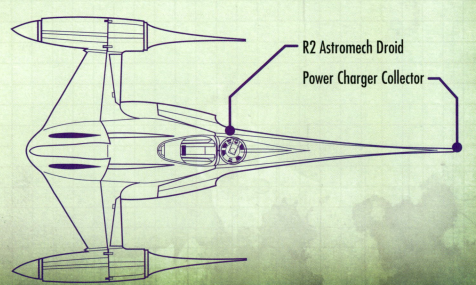

R2 Astromech Droid

Power Charger Collector

# JEDI STARFIGHTER

Designed by Kuat Systems Engineering, the Delta-7 *Aethersprite*-class light interceptor, or Jedi starfighter as it was more commonly called, flew on missions during peaceful times of the Republic. Jedi starfighters were armed with two dual laser cannons, and had room for only one pilot.

Unlike later starfighter models, the wings were too thin to accommodate a full astromech droid. Instead, a modified astromech was hardwired into a socket on the wing. Its dome remained intact but its components plugged directly into the ship's computer. The droid assisted in navigation, damage control, and hyperspace travel coordinates.

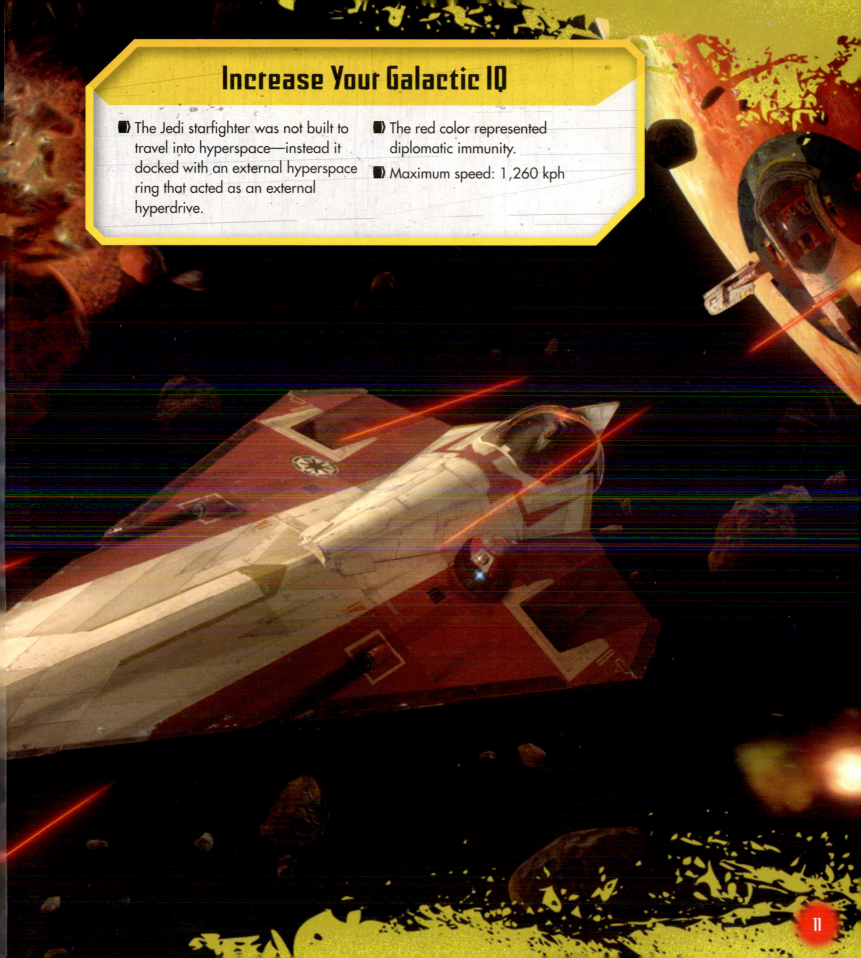

# Increase Your Galactic IQ

- The Jedi starfighter was not built to travel into hyperspace—instead it docked with an external hyperspace ring that acted as an external hyperdrive.

- The red color represented diplomatic immunity.

- Maximum speed: 1,260 kph

# REPUBLIC ASSAULT SHIP

As the Separatists were about to claim victory over the Jedi in the arena battle on Geonosis, Master Yoda arrived to save the day—along with the newly acquired clone army of the Republic. Transporting troops from Kamino, where the clones were created and trained, Republic assault ships hovered above Geonosis and unleashed an attack on the unsuspecting Separatists that many consider the beginning of the Clone Wars.

Rothana Heavy Engineering, a subsidiary of Kuat Drive Yards, designed Republic assault ships, or *Acclamator*-class transgalactic military assault ships. These giant craft boasted 12 quad laser turrets, 24 laser cannons, and 4 missile launchers. Republic assault ships proved invaluable during the Clone Wars, transporting troops to where they were needed most.

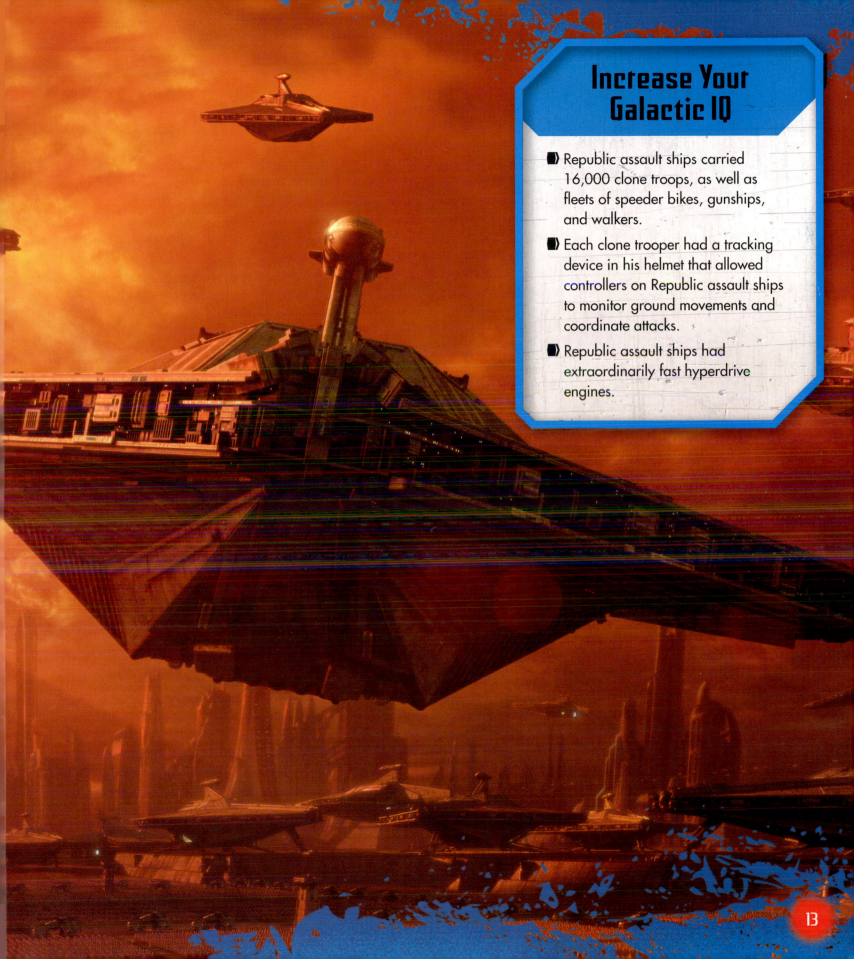

## Increase Your Galactic IQ

- Republic assault ships carried 16,000 clone troops, as well as fleets of speeder bikes, gunships, and walkers.

- Each clone trooper had a tracking device in his helmet that allowed controllers on Republic assault ships to monitor ground movements and coordinate attacks.

- Republic assault ships had extraordinarily fast hyperdrive engines.

# SOLAR SAILER

Sith Lord and Separatist leader Count Dooku flew across the galaxy in his one-of-a-kind solar sailer, a gift from the Geonosians. The ship was originally a *Punworcca 116*-class sloop, but Count Dooku instructed the Geonosians to add the solar energy–collecting sail so the ship could fly without fuel. Once the sail deployed, the absorbed energy pulled the ship through space at sublight speeds.

The ship contained a hyperdrive as well as back-up repulsor engines. Like other ships of Geonosian design, the solar sailer featured two bow prongs that extended beyond a cockpit orb. An FA-4 pilot droid did the flying while Count Dooku enjoyed his databook library. The luxurious interior featured many ornate decorations.

## Increase Your Galactic IQ

- Count Dooku fled from Geonosis in the solar sailer after a standoff with Master Yoda.
- Maximum speed: 1,600 kph
- Sail width: 112.5 meters

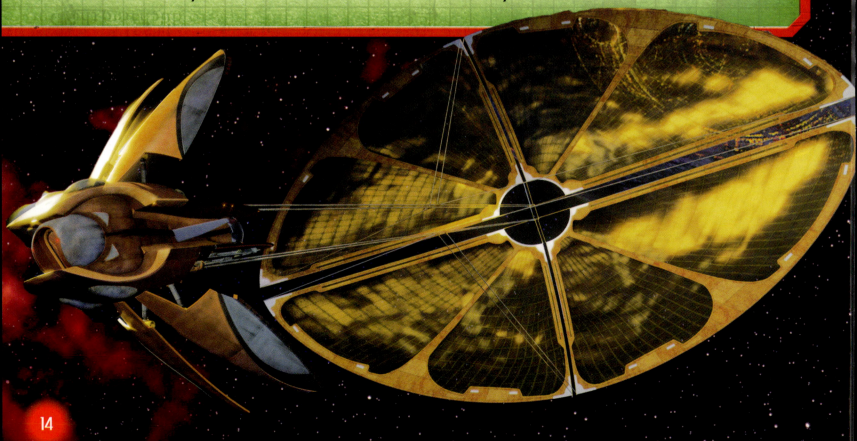

# ARC-170 FIGHTER

Created by Incom/Subpro for the Republic, the ARC-170, or Aggressive ReConnaisance fighter, was a multipurpose starship designed for intense battle as well as longer deep-space missions. The wings opened during battle to expose heat sinks and radiators to keep the ship cool. Main laser cannons located on the underside of its outer wings were uncommonly large and powerful.

The craft also had two rear-facing tail cannons as well as proton torpedoes. A crew of three—a pilot, gunner, and copilot—operated the ship, along with an astromech droid.

## Increase Your Galactic IQ

- The Republic used ARC-170 fighters heavily in the Outer Rim sieges, under the command of Generals Obi-Wan Kenobi and Anakin Skywalker.
- The nose contained long-range sensors and scanners.
- These ships played an important role in the Battle of Coruscant.
- Maximum speed: 1,050 kph

# TRI-FIGHTER

Deadly space-faring relatives of the Trade Federation's dreaded droideka, Tri-fighter starships were actually pilotless droid fighter craft developed for intense dogfighting and close-range space battles.

These droid starships were equipped with more advanced brains than standard Separatist droid fighters—and therefore were much deadlier. They came armed with four laser cannons and sinister buzz droid missiles.

## Increase Your Galactic IQ

- Buzz droid missiles did not destroy their target. Instead, they released buzz droids that landed on a target ship and drilled through its hull to dismantle it, leaving the ship adrift in space.

- During the Battle of Coruscant, a Tri-fighter launched a buzz droid missile at Obi-Wan Kenobi. Several buzz droids landed on his ship, but Anakin Skywalker and R2-D2 managed to rescue them all from the attack.

# INVISIBLE HAND

Massive and terrifying, the *Invisible Hand* played a major role in the Battle of Coruscant. A modified *Providence*-class carrier/destroyer, the Separatist Army's flagship hovered above the planet Coruscant waiting for delivery of the kidnapped Chancellor Palpatine. The Separatists planned on using the Chancellor to win the Clone Wars—but Republic ships intervened and the battle began.

Jedi Knights Obi-Wan Kenobi and Anakin Skywalker landed aboard under heavy fire from the Republic, and mounted a desperate mission to rescue the Chancellor before the ship split apart. Once they located the Chancellor, the Jedi fought their way past Count Dooku, countless battle droids and droideka, and General Grievous himself. Anakin Skywalker piloted the damaged front portion of the *Invisible Hand* to safety on the planet's surface, rescuing the Chancellor.

## Increase Your Galactic IQ

- The massive ship was armed with 14 quad laser turrets, 34 dual laser cannons, 2 ion cannons, and 102 proton torpedo launchers.
- During the rescue mission, Anakin Skywalker and Obi-Wan Kenobi flew their Jedi interceptors into the main hangar. R2-D2 plugged into the ship's computer and relayed messages to help find the Chancellor.
- Maximum speed: 2,000 kph
- Length: 1,088 meters

# JEDI INTERCEPTOR

Faster than its predecessor the *Aethersprite*, the Jedi interceptor was also smaller and more easily maneuverable in battle. Jedi used these small ships to lead their clone troops in battle during the final days of the Clone Wars.

Like earlier Jedi starfighters, these ships had no hyperdrives and relied on external hyperdrive rings to travel in deep space. These craft were also designed with sockets large enough to accommodate a complete astromech droid for navigation and repair assistance.

# Increase Your Galactic IQ

- Jedi interceptors boasted two dual laser cannons as well as two ion cannons. Unlike standard laser blasts, the ion cannons shot bursts of plasma that caused temporary electrical disruptions to their target upon impact.

- Jedi interceptor wings had upper and lower radiator panels, or s-foils, that opened to relieve excessive heat from the ship's engines. These radiator wings were opened primarily during intense fighting.

- Maximum speed: 1,500 kph

# TANTIVE IV

Owned by the Royal House of Alderaan and commanded by Captain Antilles, the *Tantive IV* flew across the galaxy on diplomatic missions as well as covert operations for the Rebel Alliance. Various symbols and red markings on its outer hull reflected its diplomatic immunity.

The ship carried Princess Leia on many successful missions. But Darth Vader overtook it above Tatooine, after the Empire suspected Princess Leia of aiding the Rebellion with theft of data tapes containing technical readouts for the Death Star.

## Increase Your Galactic IQ

- Although it was designated a diplomatic ship, the *Tantive IV* was armed with six turbolaser cannons.
- Soon after it was captured, the *Tantive IV* was destroyed by the Empire.
- Maximum speed: 950 kph

# Y-WING

Originally designed for close-quarter combat and bombing runs, the Y-wing was the Rebellion's original attack starfighter prior to the introduction of the superior X-wing. Y-wings came equipped with two laser cannons, a rotating ion cannon above the cockpit, and proton torpedo launchers.

The Y-wing was not as easily maneuvered as later rebel fighters, but its durability made sure it was present in all major battles against the Empire.

## Increase Your Galactic IQ

- Y-wings fought in the Battle of Yavin, along with X-wings.
- Astromech droid sockets were located behind the cockpit. R2 units helped Y-wing pilots with repairs and other onboard duties.
- Maximum speed: 1,000 kph

# TIE ADVANCED x1

The TIE Advanced x1 was a prototype ship that Darth Vader piloted during the Battle of Yavin. Unlike regular TIE fighters, the TIE Advanced x1 contained a hyperdrive engine and a life-support system. It also featured a shield generator, which other fighters in the Imperial fleet lacked.

The ship's wings were covered with high conversion solar panels. The wings' bent design allowed for enhanced maneuverability and speed. The x1 had a more advanced targeting system than a standard TIE fighter, making it deadly—especially when piloted by Darth Vader.

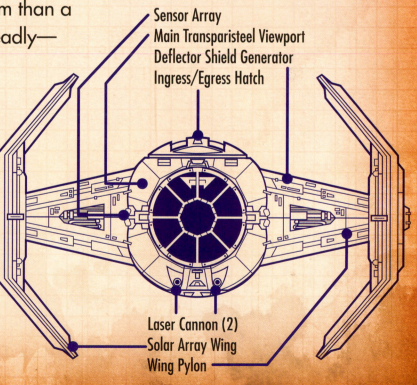

Sensor Array
Main Transparisteel Viewport
Deflector Shield Generator
Ingress/Egress Hatch

Laser Cannon (2)
Solar Array Wing
Wing Pylon

# Increase Your Galactic IQ

- At the last minute, Han Solo flew the *Millennium Falcon* into the Battle of Yavin, firing a blast that sent Darth Vader's TIE Advanced x1 spiraling out of control.
- TIE Advanced x1s proved too expensive for mass production.
- The TIE Advanced x1 carried two laser cannons.
- Maximum speed: 1,200 kph

# SUPER STAR DESTROYER
## EXECUTOR

Stationed in space outside the second Death Star during the Battle of Endor, the Super Star Destroyer *Executor* was Darth Vader's command ship and a symbol of the Empire's greed and power in the galaxy.

As part of the Emperor's plan to destroy the rebels during the battle above Endor, the *Executor* was included in an Imperial blockade to keep rebel ships from escaping. But as the battle raged on, a disabled A-wing fighter crashed into the *Executor*'s bridge, causing the Imperial behemoth to spiral out of control and crash into the surface of the Death Star.

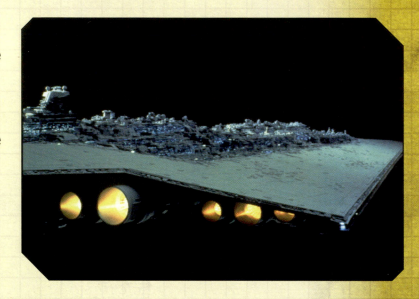

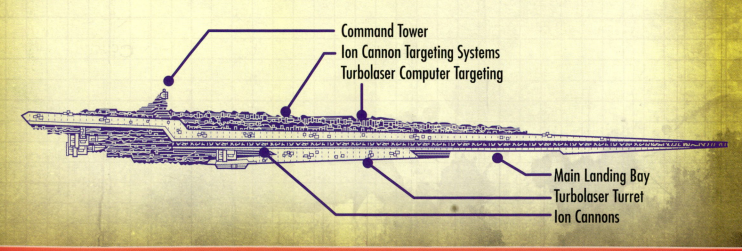

Command Tower
Ion Cannon Targeting Systems
Turbolaser Computer Targeting

Main Landing Bay
Turbolaser Turret
Ion Cannons

## Increase Your Galactic IQ

- ◗ Admiral Piett was the commanding officer on the bridge of the *Executor* during the Battle of Endor.

- ◗ The *Executor* carried a massive Imperial attack force—including TIE fighters and AT-ATs—in its docking bays.

- ◗ Length: 19,000 meters

# TIE INTERCEPTOR

This ship was created in direct response to the Rebel Alliance's introduction of faster, more effective starships.

Although slightly slower than the Rebellion's A-wing, the TIE interceptor held an advantage in maneuverability due to an ion stream projector that allowed for more complicated flight patterns, such as tight turns. Bent wings gave the ships increased power.

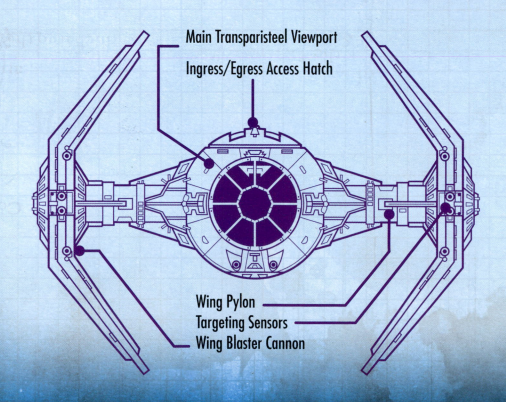

Main Transparisteel Viewport

Ingress/Egress Access Hatch

Wing Pylon
Targeting Sensors
Wing Blaster Cannon

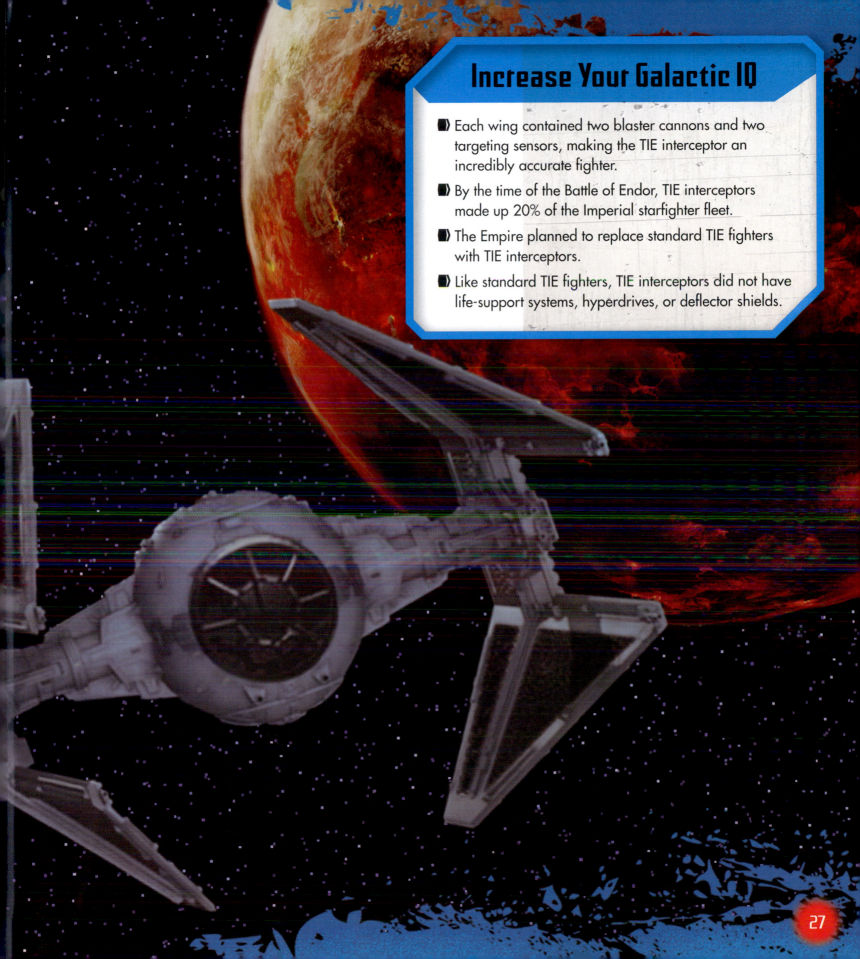

## Increase Your Galactic IQ

- Each wing contained two blaster cannons and two targeting sensors, making the TIE interceptor an incredibly accurate fighter.

- By the time of the Battle of Endor, TIE interceptors made up 20% of the Imperial starfighter fleet.

- The Empire planned to replace standard TIE fighters with TIE interceptors.

- Like standard TIE fighters, TIE interceptors did not have life-support systems, hyperdrives, or deflector shields.

# A-WING

The A-wing was the fastest starfighter in the rebel fleet, due to two specially designed engines.

These engines contained thrust-vector controls that worked with associated thruster-control jets for maneuverability in battle. To give maximum power to the engines, the ship was designed with weak shield generators and thin armor plating.

## Increase Your Galactic IQ

- A-wing controls were extremely sensitive. Only the most experienced pilots could handle these starfighters at top speed.
- A-wings played a huge part in the Rebel Alliance's success during the Battle of Endor.
- A-wings were equipped with two laser cannons.
- Length: 9.6 meters

# B-WING

The B-wing starfighter was one long wing with a cockpit at one end, and two folding airfoils that opened during flight. Heavily armed, B-wings were deadly in battle. A typical B-wing armament included two auto-blasters on the cockpit, two proton torpedo launchers at the midsection, ion cannons at the tip of each folding wing, and one laser cannon and proton torpedo launcher located at the base of the main wing.

This fighter's most important feature was its cockpit, which was surrounded by a gyrostabilization system that kept the pilot upright no matter at what angle the ship was flying.

## Increase Your Galactic IQ

◗ If the gyro surrounding the cockpit suffered damage, the B-wing would spiral out of control.

◗ The B-wing was designed so that its standard weaponry could be replaced with custom weapons, depending on its missions.

◗ Maximum speed: 950 kph

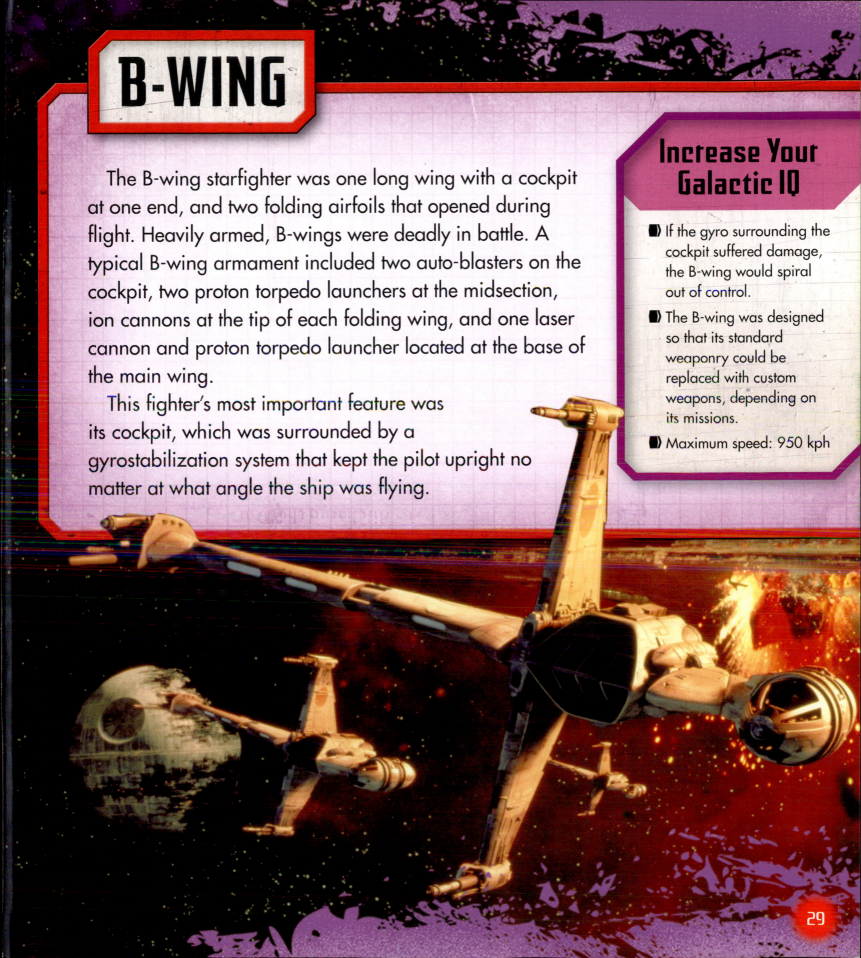

# MON CALAMARI CRUISER

Originally designed for civilian transport, these giant starships were modified for battle when the Mon Calamari donated them to the Rebel Alliance. Modifications made the cruisers especially durable in battle, in particular the overlapping shield generators. If one generator incurred damage, a nearby shield continued to protect the affected area during repairs.

*Home One* was Admiral Ackbar's command ship and the Alliance's flagship during the Battle of Endor. When Ackbar realized the Death Star was operational, he wanted to retreat. But Lando Calrissian convinced him to stall for time as the ground troops attempted to dismantle the shield generator. As the battle raged on, Admiral Ackbar ordered all rebel ships to concentrate fire on Super Star Destroyer *Executor*, ultimately leading to its destruction.

## Increase Your Galactic IQ

- *Home One* had a tractor beam, plus 36 ion cannons and 29 turbolasers.
- *Home One* housed a massive fleet of 120 starfighters.
- Length: 1,300 meters